Goat in a B
a

D0514095

L

Written by Sally Grindley
Illustrated by Mike Phillips

Ticktock

What is synthetic phonics?

Synthetic phonics teaches children to recognise the sounds of letters and to blend 'synthesise' them together to make whole words.

Understanding sound/letter relationships gives children the confidence and ability to read unfamiliar words, without having to rely on memory or guesswork; this helps them progress towards independent reading.

Did you know? Spoken English uses more than 40 speech sounds. Each sound is called a *phoneme*. Some phonemes relate to a single letter (d-o-g) and others to combinations of letters (sh-ar-p). When a phoneme is written down it is called a *grapheme*. Teaching these sounds, matching them to their written form and sounding out words for reading is the basis of synthetic phonics.

Consultant

I love reading phonics has been created in consultation with language expert Abigail Steel. She has a background in teaching and teacher training and is a respected expert in the field of Synthetic Phonics. Abigail Steel is a regular contributor to educational publications. Her international education consultancy supports parents and teachers in the promotion of literacy skills.

Reading tips

This book focuses on the oa sound as in oak.

Tricky words in this book

Any words in bold may have unusual spellings or are new and have not yet been introduced.

Tricky words in this book:

I   the   pushes
onto   into   my   they

Extra ways to have fun with this book

After the reader has finished the story, ask them questions about what they have just read:

Why does Goat get into the boat?
Where do you think the coach takes Goat and Toad?

Explain that the two letters 'oa' make one sound. Think of other words that use the 'oa' sound, such as *coat* and *float*.

Me and my friend
take turns to read.
We like reading stories
about birds best.

A pronunciation guide

This grid highlights the sounds used in the story and offers a guide on how to say them.

s as in sat	a as in ant	t as in tin	p as in pig	i as in ink
n as in net	c as in cat	e as in egg	h as in hen	r as in rat
m as in mug	d as in dog	g as in get	o as in ox	u as in up
l as in log	f as in fan	b as in bag	j as in jug	v as in van
w as in wet	z as in zip	y as in yet	k as in kit	qu as in quick
x as in box	ff as in off	ll as in ball	ss as in kiss	zz as in buzz
ck as in duck	pp as in puppy	nn as in bunny	rr as in arrow	gg as in egg
dd as in daddy	bb as in chubby	tt as in attic	sh as in shop	ch as in chip
th as in thin	th as in the	ng as in sing	nk as in sunk	le as in bottle
ai as in rain	ee as in feet	ie as in pies	oa as in oak	

Be careful not to add an 'uh' sound to 's', 't', 'p', 'c', 'h', 'r', 'm', 'd', 'g', 'l', 'f' and 'b'. For example, say 'fff' not 'fuh' and 'sss' not 'suh'.

'**I** see a coach on that road,'
croaks Toad.

'I will get on that coach,'
says Goat.

'I shall get **the** boat across the moat,' says Goat.

'Will it float?' croaks Toad.

Goat **pushes** the boat **into** the moat. Groan, groan.

Splash! The splash soaks Toad.
'**My** coat!' moans Toad.

'The boat floats!' says Goat.
'I will jump in.'

'Goat is in the boat,' croaks Toad.

'Goat is a big load!' croaks Toad.

Goat floats past a rock.
Toad jumps **onto** the rock.

Goat grins at Toad.

'I am a goat in a boat,'
boasts Goat.

Toad jumps into the boat.

The boat sinks.
'I am wet,' moans Goat.

'But Goat, I can see the coach!' croaks Toad.

Goat and Toad got on the coach.
And off **they** went!

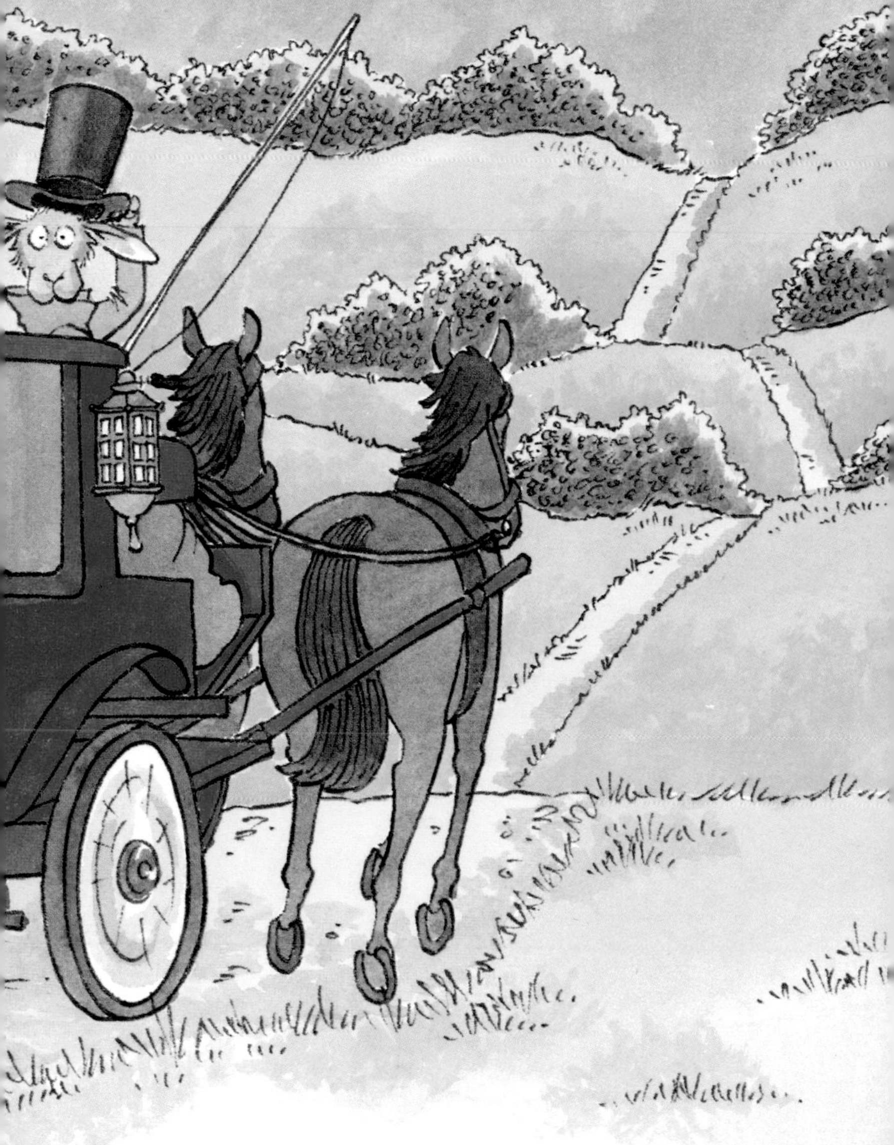

OVER 48 TITLES IN SIX LEVELS
Abigail Steel recommends...

Some titles from Level 1

Bad Rat
978-1-84898-600-8

The Best Gift
978-1-84898-603-9

Clint and Grant Play I-Spy
978-1-78325-098-1

Gran and Bret's Trip
978-1-78325-100-1

Some titles from Level 2

Wish Fish
978-1-84898-604-6

Chuck and Duck
978-1-84898-605-3

Pink Bunny
978-1-78325-103-2

Let's go to the Swings
978-1-78325-102-5

Other titles to enjoy from Level 3

Bart's Go-Cart
978-1-78325-105-6

Queen Ella's Feet
978-1-84898-609-1

Puff Flies
978-1-84898-610-7

An Hachette UK Company
www.hachette.co.uk

Copyright © Octopus Publishing Group Ltd 2012
First published in Great Britain in 2012 by TickTock, an imprint of Octopus Publishing Group Ltd,
Endeavour House, 189 Shaftesbury Avenue, London WC2H 8JY.
www.octopusbooks.co.uk
www.ticktockbooks.co.uk

ISBN 978 1 84898 611 4

Printed and bound in China
1 0 9 8 7 6 5 4 3

All rights reserved. No part of this work may be reproduced or utilised in any form or by any means, electronic or mechanical, including photocopying, recording or by any information storage and retrieval system, without the prior written permission of the publisher.